Christmas Kisses

By

Cynthia A Clement

Text copyright © 2014 Cynthia A Clement

Print Edition
ISBN: 978-1-988019-14-7

Cover Design by Melody Simmons of eBookindiecovers

Dedication

To Karen who enjoys historical romances.
Thank you for your support in both my writing
and life. I treasure your friendship always.

Chapter 1

December 1820

Charles, the sixth Earl of Stratton was a man haunted. The horror of war pursued him and his guilt was a constant burden. It was relentless in its grip. Escape was impossible.

Canon fire and the piercing screams of dying men and horses filled the air. The acrid smell of gunpowder and burning flesh stung his nostrils. His head echoed with the clashing of swords and the pounding of horses in full retreat. Battle was all around him as he lay on the ground. He looked down. He was covered in blood.

Jack's blood.

His hands trembled as he made a frantic effort to close the gaping bullet wound in Jack's chest. He couldn't let him die. The blood kept flowing through his fingers. He shouted for help, but his words were lost in the clamor of fighting. No one came to his aid. There was only him and Jack.

"Hold on." Charles's voice was hoarse.

Jack's lips twisted into a lopsided smile. "It's too late. Get out of here."

"I'm not leaving you."

"This is one journey we can't take together." Jack coughed.

Horror filled him as he watched blood seep from Jack's mouth.

"You can't die." He shook Jack's shoulders.

"It's been fun."

Jack's voice was a faint whisper as his head rolled back. He couldn't be sure if he'd actually heard the words, but that was the last sign of life in Jack. Sightless eyes stared back at him as he placed Jack's shoulders back on the ground. Charles had seen enough death in his year with the army to recognize his friend was gone.

"No."

His shriek of denial reverberated across the now empty battlefield.

The shout was loud enough to wake him from the vice grip of terror. He sat up in bed. His hands were shaking and his body was covered with sweat. It had been months since he'd had the nightmare, but it always ended the same.

Jack was dead.

He threw his covers off and pushed out of bed. Stratton Hall had triggered it. He'd hoped that coming home for Christmas would free him from his past and let him move forward with his life. Instead, it had intensified the prison that had held him captive for the past eleven years. He was usually too drunk to dream, but last night he had stopped at two glasses of port after dinner. He didn't wanted to disappoint his mother on his first visit for the holidays in eleven years.

His legs were unsteady. He walked over the lush Persian carpet to the window and threw the velvet curtain back. There was a faint orange glow of sunrise on the horizon. He put his hands against the frosted windowsill and forced himself to focus on the snow-covered vista. As far as he could see was the land of his ancestors.

His heritage.

That's what had brought him back to Stratton. He was five and thirty and should have married long ago. He owed it to his family to produce an heir, no matter how indifferent he was to the idea of marriage. His younger self had been certain he would marry for love.

The face of an angel flashed into his mind.

Helen.

It had been years since he'd allowed himself to remember. She had been breathtakingly beautiful at her debutant ball and he'd won her hand for the first waltz. Time had stood still as he held her in his arms and twirled around the ballroom. It was the last perfect moment in his life.

The next day he had sailed to war.

No point in hashing over old territory. He'd decided to wed and that's why he was here this Christmas. His bride-to-be needed to be introduced to his mother and Stratton Hall. Now that he had chosen a wife, he wanted to have the wedding as soon as possible. Waiting wasn't going to make the decision more palatable.

Lady Sybil Norbrook understood the reality of their marriage. She wasn't a starry-eyed innocent expecting love and roses. They were marrying because it was expected. He needed an heir and she wanted the position his title and money could provide. After the succession had been provided for, they were both free to go their own way as long as discretion was used.

Until then, he intended to be the perfect fiancé and husband. It was the least he could do. Sybil was willing to put up with him and he knew how difficult that was going to be. His reputation was mild in comparison to the reality of his life. He'd been honest with her about his frequent nightmares and binge drinking. That would have scared most women away long ago.

Not Lady Sybil.

She knew what she was marrying, and she didn't care.

Charles pushed away from the window. There was no point in wasting time on self-recriminations. He'd had enough years to reconcile himself to the man he was. He didn't deserve second chances or forgiveness. He was beyond redemption.

He went to his wardrobe and pulled out some leather riding breeches. He should probably wake Henson, his valet, but he'd kept the man up late last night. He, Rayburn, and Croxton had talked late into the evening. What he needed was a ride in the brisk December air. It would clear the cobwebs and doubts from his head.

Ten minutes later, he was shutting the door to his bedchamber when a squeak of the oak floorboards caught his attention. He looked down the hall. Lord Henry Croxton was moving in his direction. He was dressed in the same clothes he'd worn last night, minus his black dinner jacket and white cravat. He was dangling those over his shoulder with one finger. Charles had left Croxton drinking with Rayburn in the library the night before.

"Did you fall asleep in the chair?" The Earl didn't bother to hide his grin. He'd spent many a night passed out the same way.

"It's your fault for making them so damn comfortable."

"Blame the brandy." Stratton fell into step beside Henry, who he'd known most of his life.

They had both grown up in Derby. Henry was the younger son of the Duke of Croxton. His father was a notorious money pinch and everything had been settled on Henry's older brother Edward. Henry was frequently without funds, and Charles had pulled him out of more than one scrape in the past. He was one of the few men who had known him before the war.

"Care for a ride?"

Henry shuddered. "I need my bed."

Charles slapped him on the back. "Remember our visit to the village. Lady Sybil insists on inspecting the church before the wedding."

Henry stopped. "I thought she wanted a London marriage with all the trimmings."

"Not if we're to be wed by the New Year. My mother would like the ceremony here in the village church." Stratton shrugged. "She thinks the villagers and tenants should have a chance to see the happy couple. According to her, they've missed enough of my life and this is one way I can make up for it."

"What difference will that make? You're not staying at Stratton after the wedding."

"We'll spend some time here, especially after the children are born." Charles cleared his throat. "My mother expects it."

"At least she cares." Henry's lips twisted into a crooked smile. "I'm the spare and they've no use for me since Edward married. They're waiting for the announcement that Marion is in a family way."

"Edward's taking his time with that." They stopped in front of Henry's room. "I'll see you at luncheon."

Henry nodded and went into his bedchamber.

There was no denying that Lord Henry was handsome and that the ladies made a fuss of him, but the man was unhappy. He had a small allowance and that was likely to stop once his brother Edward, the Marquis of Bradenton, produced an heir. Henry's only prospect was a distant uncle who had promised to leave his fortune to him, but nothing more had been heard from that quarter since they were boys. Recently, Henry had been considering buying a set of colors in the Light Dragoons.

With a shrug, Charles headed down the stairs. He had enough problems of his own. Unless Henry came to him for help, he wasn't going to interfere.

The maids were already at work, brushing the stairs and cleaning out the ashes from the fireplaces. It should have given him a sense of pride that Stratton ran so smoothly, but his chest tightened and he pulled at his neck cloth. He'd spent only a few weeks here in the last eleven years. Stratton was held together by his mother. He owed her everything. Marrying to provide an heir, however unpleasant the thought, was the least he could do.

The door of the library opened and Lord Rayburn stepped out. He was a tall, dark haired man with a regal bearing. Even with wrinkled evening attire, and after a nighttime of drinking, he still had an air of distinction. He was straightening his white waistcoat, but stopped when he saw Charles.

"Must your servants be so efficient?" Rayburn stepped into the hall. "I was minding my own business and they interrupted my slumber to put more wood on the fire. A man needs privacy."

"That's why you have a bedchamber." Charles's voice was dry. "This isn't London where you sleep where you've passed out."

Rayburn raised his quizzing glass and looked Charles up and down. "Where are you going so early in the day? It's still dark."

"The sun is rising on the horizon." Charles grinned. "Join me for a ride."

"In the cold?"

"It'll clear the cobwebs."

"What if I want them to cling?" Rayburn dropped his eyeglass. "When you said we were spending the holidays in the country, you didn't mention that I'd be playing tourist."

"It's a quick tour. I promised Lady Sybil a visit into the village later in the day."

"Give me a few minutes to change."

"I'll meet you in the stables."

By the time Rayburn came down to the yard, the horses were saddled and stomping their hooves with impatience. Within seconds, they were astride the animals and galloping across the east lawn. They headed away from Stratton Hall. It was several minutes before they slowed to a canter. The house was no longer visible and they had entered the home wood. They followed a trail that led through the large snow covered oak trees and pines until they reached a road on the other side.

Charles pulled up his horse and stopped.

"Where does this go?" Lord Rayburn gestured to the road.

"To the village." He pointed to the right, his breath forming a frozen vapor as he spoke. "The opposite direction leads to some of the tenant farmsteads."

"Shall we?" Rayburn galloped in the opposite direction of the village.

The next two hours were spent inspecting farms before heading back to Stratton Hall. As they approached the sand-colored stone mansion, a surge of pride flooded Charles. This was his home and even though he had avoided visiting, the memory of it was with him always.

They left the horses with the grooms and started toward the house. For the first time since the war, he felt a glimmer of hope. Soon he would be married, and after that, children.

Focusing on the future might reduce the sting of his misery.

"Is Lady Sybil serious about marrying on New Year's Day?" Rayburn's voice interrupted his thoughts.

Charles nodded. "She says that she's past the age of wanting a fairy-tale wedding. The sooner we are wed, the sooner we can begin our family."

Rayburn slapped him on the back. "I never thought I'd see the day you'd give up your freedom."

The Earl grinned. "It's our duty to provide heirs."

Rayburn cleared his throat. "I have a few more years before I have to worry about that."

Beaton, the butler, opened the door before they had reached the top stair. "Lady Sybil has requested you meet her in the drawing room."

"Already she notices your absence. Imagine the delights that await once you're married." There was a hint of mockery in Rayburn's voice.

"It will be your turn one day."

Rayburn shuddered and waved his farewell as he climbed the stairs.

Charles pulled off his hat and gloves and handed them to Beaton. "Tell Lady Sybil I'll be there after I've changed from my riding clothes."

Beaton cleared his throat. "If I might be so bold, my lord?"

Charles had been absent from Stratton for a number of years, but he recognized the disapproval in Beaton's voice. It was a tone that had often been directed at him when he was a boy. He put his hands behind his back and nodded. There was no point in avoiding the problem.

"Lady Sybil was insistent that you see her the moment you crossed the threshold." Beaton closed the door. "It might be expedient to acquiesce to her wishes."

It sounded as if Sybil had set the house on its ears. There was no point in giving the servants more to gossip about. The sooner he saw her, the better. At the drawing room entrance he straightened his shoulders before pushing the door open.

Sunlight streamed into the room from the bank of windows along the south side. His mother had draped the room in chintz floral and deep red solids. The sofas and chairs were done in matching greens and there was a liberal sprinkling of family antiques from the sixteenth and seventeenth century. He'd always found the room comforting. It complimented Lady Sybil's coloring, which was probably why she'd chosen to meet him here.

His fiancée was as beautiful as ever, with her auburn hair dressed elegantly atop her head. She was tall and willowy, suggesting a fragile woman. Her looks were deceiving. She was strong willed, with a temper that had sent many a lesser man running. Right now her emerald eyes were flashing sparks at him and her lips were pursed.

"What's so important that you couldn't wait for me to change?" He brushed snow from his jacket. "I smell of the stables."

"Have you no honor?"

Charles's eyes narrowed. "You have me at a disadvantage."

"I won't tolerate this behavior once we're married." Lady Sybil crossed her arms over her chest.

He pinched his nose. "What am I accused of?"

"I know you've got a woman here. I overheard the servants discussing it."

"They were misinformed." Stratton forced his voice to remain calm. "I haven't visited the estate above five times in the last eleven years."

"That's a lie. You've allowed this woman to live in one of your cottages." Lady Sybil's voice rose to a shrill. "Who is Helen?"

A stab of pain clenched at his chest and Charles forced himself to breath. "She is the sister of one of my best friends."

"Only a woman totally beyond the pale would agree to let a man keep her." Sybil's voice was a low snarl. "We both know that is the company you prefer."

"I won't have you besmirch her reputation with your allegations." His voice rose. "You know nothing about her situation."

"No genteel woman would live on her own. Why is she not living in her brother's house?"

"He's dead." Charles spat the words out. "And I'm the reason he was killed."

Chapter 2

Helen Bryant was twenty-nine, unmarried, and content with her life. She'd spent the last eleven years raising her younger sisters. Love had directed her choices, not duty. Now that her youngest sister was married, she was free to pursue her own desires. Most women her age would have bemoaned the fact that they were a spinster, but she had refused to settle for a husband. Love was the only reason she would marry.

"They're here." Georgette's excited voice rang through the church.

Helen paused in her decorating and looked down the aisle. Georgette was jumping up and down and clapping her hands. Not yet sixteen, Georgette hadn't completely lost the enthusiasm of a child. That would come soon enough. Next year she'd be making her formal entrance into society with her debut in London.

Marriage wouldn't be far behind, especially with her blonde hair and blue eyed innocence. After seeing three younger sisters comfortably wed, Helen knew what men were attracted to in a wife. Besides looks and a fortune, Georgette had a sweetness of disposition which was rare. Men would be falling over themselves to win her hand.

"Who's coming?" Helen turned back to her flowers, nestling the final carnation in place.

"The Earl."

Her heart stuttered to a stop.

Then it began to race.

Three years had passed since she'd last seen him. It had been a chance meeting in the village. She'd been taking a basket of food to Mrs. McAdams, who was bedridden, and the Earl had been leaving the inn. They'd come face to face on the roadway. She still cringed when she remembered Stratton's reaction.

She'd asked him about his estate and his plans. The Earl had pulled at his cravat and looked at his pocket watch. Seconds later, he'd tipped his hat and left. After all these years, he still couldn't face her. It wouldn't hurt so much if she didn't love him.

She'd fallen in love with Charles when she was sixteen.

Her love was still strong despite his indifference.

There was no point in dwelling on something she couldn't change. She lived a full life and there was no room in it for self-recriminations or pity. She hung the cedar across the altar and stepped back to look at the finished decorations. She tilted her head and wondered if the boughs overwhelmed the flowers.

"Afraid that it won't meet Reverend Black's approval?"

Helen's breath caught in her throat as her gaze fell upon Stratton.

The years had been kind to him. The layers of his caped coat added bulk to his already tall and muscular frame and there was no gray in his blonde locks. The difference was in his eyes. They were still a deep chocolate brown, but there was no warmth in them. There was a hard set to his jaw and his lips were a tight line. No welcoming smile, only a nod.

He was standing in the aisle with a group of people. Three ladies dressed in London finery, and two gentlemen. She recognized one of the men as Lord Henry Croxton, but the rest were strangers. The youngest, and by far the prettiest woman, was clinging to Stratton's arm. She was tall with reddish brown hair. Her real beauty was her eyes, emerald green and sparking fire. Even without introductions Helen knew who she was.

Lady Sybil Norbrook.

Stratton's fiancée.

"Reverend Black always likes Helen's decorations." Georgette's defensive voice echoed in the old stone church. She slapped a hand over her mouth. "I'm sorry. I meant Miss Bryant."

Helen laughed. "It's alright Georgette. The Earl and I are acquainted."

Lady Sybil's eyes narrowed. "I'm certain things are more informal in small villages, but introductions would be proper for the rest of us."

"Forgive me." Stratton made a slight bow. "Lady Sybil Norbrook, allow me introduce you to Miss Bryant. I've known her since she was a baby."

"She looks too old for that." Lady Sybil's voice grated.

Lady Sybil's words were met with silence. A muscle in Stratton's jaw clenched. One of the other gentlemen cleared his throat, but there was a twinkle in his eyes. Helen fought the urge to chuckle. It was a ridiculous situation. She had no intention of fencing words with Lady Sybil.

"I'm afraid I'm rather disheveled this morning. These clothes were chosen for function, not fashion." She brushed a hand down her worn brown gown. "We went out early to gather the boughs."

"That's no excuse for rudeness." Stratton's voice was harsh. "I believe Lady Sybil owes you an apology."

Lady Sybil straightened her shoulders. "It was an honest mistake."

"I don't offend easily." Helen's voice was soft. "Stratton and my brother were the best of friends when they were growing up. It's been years since we last met, but I'm happy to see the Earl back home. Everyone was pleased to hear about your upcoming nuptials."

"Very prettily put." One of the gentlemen stepped forward and bowed. "Stratton is being remiss with introductions. I am Lord Rayburn."

Helen curtsied. "It's a pleasure to meet you."

Rayburn was a tall dark-haired man with laughing grey eyes. His reputation, as a rake and hellhound, was legendary. He was almost as notorious as the Earl for drinking and gambling. Mothers warned their daughters away from him, despite his enormous wealth.

"I've known Stratton for over eight years and he's never mentioned anything about his youth, least of all knowing such a beauty as yourself."

"You flatter me, Lord Rayburn." Her lip twitched up at the corner. "Even here in the wilds of Derby, we've heard of you."

"Lies, I'm sure." Rayburn grinned. "Why have I not met you before?"

"I'm seldom in London." Helen gathered her basket close. "I have no reason to travel nowadays and I prefer village life. Let me introduce Miss Georgette Wishert."

"The village would be lost without Miss Bryant." Georgette stood close to her. "She helps where it's needed."

"The advantage of not having a family of her own. It's wonderful that she is able to give to others." Lady Sybil's voice was sweet, but her eyes shot darts at Helen.

Helen tilted an eyebrow. She'd been willing to forgive Lady Sybil for mistaking her appearance, but to suggest that she had no family was going too far. She tightened her hold on her basket. She was about to correct the lady when Stratton spoke.

"Miss Bryant raised her sisters after her brother's death." Stratton's voice was devoid of emotion. "Her parents had died a year earlier."

"How sad." Lord Rayburn's voice was casual. He glanced at Stratton and then back at her. "How old were you."

"Eighteen." Stratton answered for her. His voice was clipped. "Let me finish with the introductions. This is Lady Alice Rayburn, Nigel's sister. Beside her is Lady Sybil's sister, Lady Holsten, and lastly Lord Henry Croxton, who you already know.

Lady Rayburn was similar in looks to her brother, but much younger. Her air of polish equaled Lady Sybil's. The two women appeared to be close friends judging by the looks they kept sharing. Lady Holsten was an older version of her sister. Lord Henry was dark and brooding. Handsome was an understatement when used to describe him. He had grown up in the county and even though it had been years since she'd seen him, she would have recognized him anywhere.

Helen and Georgette made their curtsies. "It has been a delight meeting you, but it's time I returned Georgette to her home. Her father will be worried."

"Not if I'm with you." Georgette picked up her gloves that she'd left on one of the pews. "He trusts you completely."

"Before you lovely ladies leave, haven't you forgotten something?" Lord Rayburn's voice was light with reproof.

Helen glanced around the church. The ancient stone walls were decorated with plaques that commemorated the deeds of valor of the parishioners over the last nine centuries. Everywhere she looked there were boughs of holly and pine. Cedar and pine cone wreaths hung from the ends of the time worn oak pews.

A small nativity scene was at the front of the church. All of the statues were in their place except baby Jesus. He would be laid in the crèche by one of the children of the parish on Christmas Eve. There didn't seem to be anything out of place.

With a frown she turned back to Lord Rayburn. "Enlighten us."

"Mistletoe."

Georgette clapped her hands. "Of course. It's exactly what we need."

Helen laughed. "Not in the church. Perhaps in Stratton Hall for the village fete."

"Is there to be a party at the Hall?" Lady Sybil's eyes narrowed. "Why wasn't I informed?"

"My mother takes care of it." Stratton shifted on his feet.

"Lady Stratton relies on Miss Bryant for help." Georgette's voice was defensive. "We're going to decorate the Hall tomorrow."

"That will change now that I'm here." Lady Sybil put her hand on Stratton's arm. "I've seen enough. I want to return to the Hall."

The Earl gave a slight bow of his head. "Ladies." Then he escorted his guests out of the church.

Silence followed their departure.

Helen picked up her gloves. "It's time we were on our way also."

"I should have guessed that you knew Lord Stratton." Georgette's voice was apologetic. "I've never met an Earl before."

Helen pushed the fingers of her gloves tight to her hand. "You weren't living in the village then. He and my brother Jack were great friends."

They left the church, shutting the door behind them. It was late afternoon and the sky had a leaden look to it. Soon there would be snow. Helen inhaled the crisp air and let it cool her body and thoughts. Charles had chosen his bride. She would hope and pray he'd be happy.

"What did you think of Lady Sybil?" Georgette's voice was cautious.

Helen pulled her brown spencer closer. "She'll make him a perfect Countess. She's already making plans to take over the annual Christmas fete."

"That's because she's jealous."

"Perhaps." Helen walked in the direction of Georgette's home. "I've found it never pays to question someone's motivation. It hurts less."

When they reached the Wishert house, Georgette's father opened the door. It was one of the first grand houses built in the village and was done in the Tudor style. Georgette's father had bought it eight years earlier when he'd retired from industry. He'd made a fortune for himself with trade and had decided to settle his family in the village of Fritchly to focus on raising his only child. His wife had never been strong, so the retirement had been a blessing. Mrs. Wishert's health had recovered enough that she was able to watch over their daughter's lessons now.

"I was ready to come searching for you." Mr. Wishert's voice boomed from the entry. "Did the Reverend have some special requests?"

"You'll never guess who we met?" Georgette's voice rose in excitement. "The Earl and his fiancée, Lady Sybil Norbrook."

"That's a surprise. Stratton's seldom here."

"Helen knows him."

"Ah, that makes sense lassie. Miss Bryant grew up here." Wishert ushered his daughter into the house. "Go and tell your mother the news."

"We finished the church decorations." Helen's voice was warm. She liked Mr. Wishert, who was a generous father and friend. "Georgette was a great help."

"I'm glad for it." Wishert rubbed his nose. "I hope she didn't pester you too much."

"It's a pleasure being around Georgette."

"Stay for tea. The Missus has it ready in the drawing room."

"Are you certain?"

"My wife is having one of her better days and we'd be honored if you'd visit."

Helen handed her basket and spencer to the butler and followed Mr. Wishert into the drawing room. Georgette and her mother were already sitting on the sofa with a tea tray in front of them. The fire was lit and the room was a welcomed warmth after the chill of the unheated church. She sat across from them and accepted a cup of tea with a fresh baked scone.

An hour later Mr. Wishert escorted her to the door. "I'll pick up Georgette in the morning. We still have the Hall decorations to attend to."

Helen stepped outside. The wind had picked up and she pulled her spencer closer.

"It looks like snow." Georgette's father glanced up at the grey sky. "I'll send my coach to pick you up and take you to the Hall tomorrow."

"That's very kind." Helen turned. "Tell Georgette I'll see her in the morning."

She walked along the frozen roadway that ran through the village. It was a familiar route. One that she could travel in her sleep, but she had no wish to be out in the dark. The sun was setting lower in the sky, so she hastened her steps. Molly, her housemaid was used to her arriving home late, but she worried until Helen walked through the door. She was within sight of her cottage before she noticed a figure walking his horse in front of her fence. It took her a second to recognize her visitor.

Charles, the Earl of Stratton.

It was too late for a social call, so it must be important. She picked up her skirts and started to run. Her foot slipped on the dusting of snow covering the road, but she recovered and kept moving. By the time she reached the gate her breath was coming in gasps.

"Is something wrong at the Hall?"

He shook his head. "No."

She sagged against the fence. "Why are you here?"

"We need to talk."

Chapter 3

"It's late." A small tendril of longing curled deep within Helen. It was dangerous to her peace of mind to continue speaking with Charles alone.

"I wanted to apologize."

"For what?" She straightened and opened her gate.

"Lady Sybil was rude at the church."

"You could have told me that tomorrow."

The Earl motioned in the direction of Stratton Hall. "You're on the edge of the estate and I wanted to talk to you in private."

She hesitated. Charles was fidgeting with his horse's reins. He looked down at his feet and then over his shoulder. She remembered how he had done the same thing when they were kids and he was unsure. Deep within her heart, the part she kept protected, a crack started. Even after all this time, she couldn't resist him.

"I haven't seen you for more than two minutes together in the last eleven years and suddenly, twice in one day."

"I didn't know what to say."

"I've never known you to be at a loss for words." She clutched her basket close to her chest. She didn't bother to hide the exasperation in her voice. He couldn't waltz back into her life and not expect her to react.

"Can I come in?"

Helen glanced at her door and then back at the Earl. "Is that wise?"

"I'll risk it." He gave her a lopsided grin that twisted at her heart.

"You're the landlord." Helen walked through the gate. "Thank you for letting us stay at the cottage. It made things easier for me and my sisters."

He tied his horse to a fence post and followed her to the door. "I'm glad I was able to do something right."

His derisive tone made her glance up at him. "I have no complaints. Having a place to stay meant I could keep the family together."

"My mother wrote me that your cousin wasn't accommodating."

Helen led the Earl into the small room that served as their drawing room. The cottage was made of thick stone that showed through to the interior walls. Over the years they had put up tapestries, and small samplers to add warmth to the room, but nothing could hide the age of the furniture. She ran a hand over the well-worn fabric of one of the chairs.

"We had few choices after Jack's death." She undid her spencer and put it over the basket she had placed on an oak side table. "The new baron and his wife claimed there was no room at the estate for us."

Charles went to the fireplace and stood with his hands behind his back. "That's why I had to intervene."

"I appreciated it." She sat across from him. "Your man of business thought you had ulterior motives."

"I was still recovering in London when I heard that you had no home." A muscle tightened in his jaw. "It was the least I could do."

"Your mother told us that you were several months recuperating."

"Eight to be exact." He grimaced. "A bullet shattered my leg. It was only my stubbornness that prevented the surgeon from amputating."

Charles was the picture of health and physique. "Is that why you stayed away?"

"In the beginning." The Earl flexed his right leg. "It took me over two years to walk properly."

"Most men would have wanted to recover in the country."

"There was nothing here for me." His voice was clipped.

Helen clenched her hands together. His words stung like a slap across the face. The anguish of Charles's rejection was a familiar ache, though. She took a deep breath and straightened her shoulders.

"Not even your mother?"

"She would have fussed." His tone was low. "It was bad enough I was an invalid. I didn't need my mother's disappointment too."

"You're healed now." She kept her voice soft. "Surely you could have visited more often?"

"I came when necessary." His voice was defensive. "My estate is well run. My life is in London."

Helen held his gaze. "Are you happy?"

For a second, a flicker of agony crossed his face before his lips twisted with derision. "My days are full."

"We do hear tales." She kept her voice devoid of emotion.

"I see no point in moderation." Stratton's tone was hard.

Her chest tightened. This man was very different from the one who'd gone away to war. Pain and death had changed him. She longed to hold him close and ease his burden, but his rigid stance warned her that he didn't want her sympathy or her love.

"What's the real reason you came to see me?"

"I wanted the thank you for helping my mother over the years." Stratton cleared his throat. "Especially with the Christmas celebrations."

"I enjoy helping." She settled back in her chair. "It's a shame you've been unable to make it home for the past few years."

He gave a short laugh. "It's more than a few years."

"Eleven to be exact." She didn't hide her criticism. "I can understand having a full life in London, but there is no excuse for not returning for Christmas."

"It didn't seem right to celebrate without Jack." The Earl's jaw clenched. "The last Christmas we spent together was in Spain. We were in full retreat to the coast. There was mud, rain, and chaos everywhere, yet we found an abandoned shed and carved out a day of peace and joy."

Helen's throat tightened. "Jack loved Christmas."

"It was his favorite time of year." Charles nodded. "He'd pick out the tree he wanted in July and we'd have to visit it every day to be certain it was still standing. Do you remember the year your father cut down a different pine?"

"Jack was so upset." A glow of remembered happiness filled her. "After that Jack always brought home the tree."

"He'd cut the tree, but I had to drag it back to your house."

Charles smiled. A wide jubilant grin that lit his face. Her breath caught in her throat at the sight. The last time she'd seen him so carefree had been at her debutant ball when he'd cut in front of one of her other suitors and claimed her hand for a waltz. He'd been the triumphant hero.

"I feel Jack closest during the holidays. I know he's always with me, but it's different at Christmas." Her voice was a low whisper.

"I only feel his loss."

A rush of sympathy and understanding filled Helen. "So you stayed away."

"It eased the torment." He cleared his throat. "I can't live in the past, though. I will be married soon and that means spending more time at Stratton."

"The villagers and your tenants will be happy."

"What about you?"

"You belong at Stratton Hall." Her voice was sincere.

Charles nodded. "I want you and Sybil to get along. She's a headstrong woman, but I know your help will ease her transition. People will accept her if you're seen to be friends."

"I can't guarantee that." She bit her lower lip. "She has taken me in dislike."

He gave her a wry look. "She overheard the servants speaking about you and the cottage."

"And jumped to the wrong conclusion."

"I explained the circumstances." Stratton tugged at his cravat. "In time she'll see that you're not a threat."

"I can't continue to live here."

"Nonsense. I gave the cottage to you for as long as you want." His voice was firm. "Sybil will have to accept it."

"I'll try to help Lady Sybil, for your sake." Helen stood. "You'll miss dinner up at the Hall if you stay much longer. Is there anything else you needed to say to me?"

"No." He moved to the door. "Until tomorrow."

She walked him outside and waited until he'd mounted his horse and rode off, before shutting the door. She leaned back against it and shut her eyes for a brief second before pushing away and walking to the kitchen.

The chill of the outside didn't compete with the one inside her heart. She'd given up any hope of Charles returning her love years ago. She'd accepted that she would spend her life alone, but seeing him again had stirred up hopes. Crazy, insane dreams of love and romance. It wasn't meant to be. He was marrying another woman.

Loving Charles had been the one constant in her life.

He was the only man who made her heart beat fast and her breath catch in her throat. A look from him had made her body burn for things she didn't understand. Throughout the years of raising her sisters and seeing them settled, there had always been the hope that she'd find someone else who affected her like Charles. It hadn't happened.

She had a wide range of male friends, but none of them made her pulse quicken. She had a small portion and with her sisters married, she lived quite comfortably. She was old enough that society wouldn't censor her for living on her own. She'd accepted that she would only love one man and had been content until today. She had believed she was free of her girlhood fantasies and was a woman at peace with her life. Now she knew differently.

It was impossible for her to remain living so close to the man she loved and see him married to another. The torture of it would be worse than never seeing him again. There was only one sensible thing to do.

She had to leave the area.

Chapter 4

Charles leaned back in his chair. His mother, the Countess of Stratton, was sitting beside him in the library. She was reading aloud a list of duties that he was expected to perform at the annual Christmas fete. She turned the page and continued, looking up at him with the occasional expectant look.

He frowned.

His mother's voice had been a backdrop to his thoughts. He'd been contemplating Helen Bryant. She must be nine and twenty now, but her looks were still vibrant. She was a beautiful woman. Dark hair, without a trace of gray, framed her perfectly proportioned face. Her deep blue eyes were always filled with laughter, except when she'd spoken of Jack last night. He forced his mind away from that memory.

"Why didn't Helen marry?" Charles interrupted his mother.

His mother folded her list. "It's not because of lack of opportunity."

"What's that supposed to mean?"

"You're the only man in the county who hasn't asked her to marry him."

A jolt of disbelief shot through him. "She's Jack's younger sister."

"You say that as if it were a sin. Helen isn't your sister." His mother frowned. "She's a beautiful woman who faced tragedy and survived. Even when she had the opportunity to make life easier, she refused to compromise."

"Compromise in what way?"

"Bessington offered for her."

He sat forward. The Duke of Bessington would have been a feather in any young lady's cap. He was middle aged and had outlived two wives, but he had wealth and position. Despite his reputation of being bad tempered, most women would have jumped at his offer of marriage.

"When?"

"It was just after Jack's funeral." Lady Stratton shook her head. "His offer would have solved her problems. I don't know how she managed to keep things together on her own."

"Why is this the first time I'm hearing about it?"

"You've never asked before." There was a hint of reproach in his mother's voice. "You were in so much grief over Jack's death that the rest of the world disappeared."

Charles snorted. "You mean I was a self-absorbed, egocentric prig."

"That's not what I said." His mother touched his arm. "You blamed yourself for Jack's death. I'm glad to see you're moving forward with your life."

"Because of my engagement?" He stretched his legs out in front of him. "I know my duty to the family."

"I was referring to you being home for Christmas. It's the first time since the war." His mother's voice held exasperation. "I would like to discuss your marriage, though. Why the rush?"

"It was long overdue." He raised an eyebrow. "Lady Sybil is eminently suitable. You can't have any objections on that front."

"She has the right connections." His mother cleared her throat. "Do you love her?"

Stratton straightened up in his chair. "What does love have to do with marriage?"

"Everything." Lady Stratton rolled her list between her fingers. "You're my son. I want to see you happy."

"I need an heir."

"You need love." His mother leaned forward. "If she makes you happy, then I'm glad."

"We suit each other." Charles pushed away his feelings of distaste. "She understands that I'm not the kind of man to fall in love. We will deal well together."

"That sounds cold and unemotional."

"I'm a realist." He stood. "I want an heir and she wants a position in society."

His mother sighed. "I wish you well. It's not what I would have chosen for you, but it's your life."

He clenched his jaw. "It's necessary. I've had more than enough time to find love."

"You've looked in the wrong places." His mother held up a hand when he started to speak. "I know all about your life in London. You wouldn't recognize love if it was standing in front of you."

Charles's eyes widened at the sternness in his mother's voice. She left the room before he could reply. He'd been disappointing her for years and it was no surprise that she had heard rumors of his life in London. He lived like many of the young bucks of the ton. His days were spent riding and sporting, his nights drinking, gambling, and womanizing. It gave him respite from the grief he carried. He couldn't change who he was. Life had made him that way.

He walked to the window and looked out over his grounds. He rubbed a hand over the familiar tightness in his chest. He hadn't enjoyed being at Stratton Hall since the war. Too many memories and regrets. He pushed away from the window. He was about to leave, when there was a knock at the door.

"Come."

Lady Sybil walked in. "I think it would be best if we straightened a few things out."

"By all means." Stratton motioned her to the chair his mother had just vacated. "What seems to be the problem?"

"You know very well." Sybil sat. "I want you to be honest about Miss Bryant. What does she mean to you?"

"Helen? I thought we settled that yesterday." He laughed. "Don't tell me you're jealous?"

"Of that old spinster?" Lady Sybil tossed her head. "She can't compete with me. It's not right that another woman is doing the duties reserved for the lady of the house."

"You'll handle things once you're my wife."

Charles's voice was dry. Lady Sybil seldom did anything more than necessary. She was a social butterfly and ambitious. That's why they would deal well together. Once she'd given him an heir, they'd go their separate ways.

"Is there anything else you wish to discuss?"

Sybil's eyes narrowed. "You two seem to be on familiar terms. Your reputation has been well-earned. You've bedded most of the ton and I won't have one of your former lovers living on our doorstep."

Anger ripped through him. His reputation was beyond repair. He was a rakehell that very few men could compete with. He tainted everything he touched in his life, but he had never touched Helen. That would have been the ultimate crime.

"I've already denied a relationship between us. Your persistence is ridiculous." His tone was harsh. "Have a care. I won't tolerate a wife who doubts my word."

"Don't get me started on what I expect from a husband or we'd be here all day." Sybil smoothed her hand over her skirt. "She is one of your tenants. She cannot remain at Stratton."

Stratton raised an eyebrow. "I have hundreds of tenants. Surely you're not asking me to evict all of them?"

"If they're attractive women you have a history with? Yes."

"I have no personal history with Helen other than I grew up with her older brother." He crossed his arms. "There's no reason for jealousy."

Sybil pursed her lips. "I don't expect you to be faithful, but I won't have your mistresses flaunted under my nose."

"You paint a lovely picture of our marriage." Charles didn't hide his sarcasm. "I'll do my best to keep my affairs discrete. I expect the same of you."

"That goes without saying." Sybil's voice was curt.

"You never miss a chance for romance."

"This is a marriage of convenience. You need a wife and I need a man who can provide me with a social position."

"We understand each other perfectly, but I won't have a wife who thinks she can control my actions."

"Discretion is what I demand." Sybil stood and straightened her gown. "Step over that line and I will make your life hell."

"You almost convince me that we won't suit."

"I won't be jilted." Sybil's voice took on a tone of steel. "Your reputation couldn't stand the damage my family would put it through."

He turned away from her and walked to the window. "There's no chance of that happening. Unless you decide that we won't suit, we'll be married at the end of the year as planned."

"Good."

He listened to the rustle of skirts and then the slamming of the library door. God, what a mess he'd gotten himself into. He could have had his pick of the young debutantes last season, but their innocence and insipid conversation bored him. He was too tainted by life to sully another person. Sybil had been on the town for several seasons and knew the score.

Her family had a heritage that went back generations. She wanted a husband with a title and position. He wanted a wife who had no expectations of him. It had seemed perfect. Almost a match made in heaven.

He snorted and turned away from the window. He was wasting time. He'd promised Rayburn a ride. Anything to get away from the slow pace of country life. He started toward the door, but a crisp rap and a twist of the handle stopped him.

Rayburn entered.

"I was coming to find you." Charles straightened his jacket. "Are you ready for another tour of the estate?"

"Later." Rayburn grinned. "A delightful group of young ladies has invaded the hall."

"You've always insisted that the young are a bore."

"They are." Rayburn closed the door behind him. "But when a beautiful older chaperon accompanies them, all bets are off."

Stratton frowned. "Who?"

"The delightful Miss Bryant."

His chest tightened. "Helen is off limits."

Rayburn's eyes narrowed. "In all of the years I've known you, no woman has been off limits."

"She's the sister of my best friend." Charles forced his heart beat to slow.

Rayburn rested against his desk. "The friend I've never heard you mention."

"Jack Bryant."

"Tell me about him."

Stratton shrugged. "He died eleven years ago. There's not much else to tell."

"How old was he?"

"Twenty-three." Charles cleared his throat. "He died at the Battle of Corunna."

"The same battle you were injured at?"

He nodded. "We joined together."

"So he died and you lived?" Rayburn was silent for several seconds. "That explains how you know Miss Bryant, but not why you've never mentioned her."

"Do you tell me about all of your beautiful acquaintances?"

"Yes." Rayburn laughed. "I could never keep someone as delectable as Miss Bryant a secret"

"She's not on the menu." His voice was harsher than he'd intended.

Rayburn rubbed his chin. "It's like that is it?"

Stratton started toward the door. "She deserves respect. Keep clear."

Rayburn raised his hands in a conciliatory gesture. "I promise. You can't stop me from conversing with her, though."

"I wouldn't dream of it." Charles opened the door.

"Good." Rayburn pushed ahead of him. "She's the only thing keeping this holiday interesting."

"I thought you wanted to have an old fashioned Christmas."

"I'd forgotten what a bore they are."

"It's only for a fortnight."

Charles led the way to the main hall. It was the original great room when the castle had been a stronghold in Norman times. Centuries of renovations and additions had turned what had been a utilitarian fortress, into a family home. Oak panelling, large tapestries, and family portraits covered the walls. A central staircase led to the upper floors. Additional wings had been added over the centuries, but he felt most connected in the original hall. It was where his ancestors had conducted business and met with their tenants for centuries.

The Christmas party was to be held in the ballroom. It had been added to the house a hundred years earlier and had been built off the main hall. When they reached the room they were confronted by several young girls giggling and stringing mistletoe from the chandeliers. He tried to hide his smile, but their joy was contagious. It had been years since he'd allowed himself to experience the Christmas festivities. Perhaps this year he would make peace with the season.

"Look." Miss Georgette Wishert pointed at the hanging mistletoe. "Do you think we need more?"

"There are plenty of opportunities to catch a kiss in this room." Charles looked up at the ceiling. "You'll have everyone tripping over themselves to avoid it."

Georgette bit her lip. "Is it too much?"

"Never." Rayburn stepped forward and took Georgette by the elbow and led her to the center of the room. "There's none on the dancing floor and that is the most important thing. It would be a disaster to interrupt the dancers."

Georgette giggled. "You're teasing me."

Rayburn gave a slight bow. "Is that what I'm doing?"

"Some might call it flirting." Helen's voice was matter of fact.

Georgette's eyes widened. "Is that true?"

"I was serious." Rayburn's eyes twinkled.

Charles bit his tongue. His friend was a notorious womanizer, but he usually drew the line at girls still in the schoolroom. It must be the festive atmosphere. Everywhere boughs of cedar and pine were strewn along the walls, the mantle, and across the doorways. The place smelled more of the forest than the outside did.

"I think the room looks wonderful." He put his hands behind his back. "You're to be commended for a superb job. Everyone in the village will be enchanted."

Helen finished intertwining a bough of cedar with the pine rope that was adorning the mantle of the large marble fireplace. She stepped back to assess the finished product and Charles's eyes lingered on her. His mother was right. She was no longer the young girl he remembered. She was a woman. A very beautiful woman, with curves in all the right places. A stir of attraction drew him closer.

"It looks magnificent."

"I want it to be perfect. It's your first Christmas at home in years." Helen fussed with the cedar branches.

He grimaced. "This is for the guests, not me."

She looked at him with wide eyes. "It's your home and a reflection on you."

"The tenants will be more concerned about whether I intend to stay."

"You took care of the estate." Helen stepped back from the fireplace.

"I know my duty."

"They want to celebrate you being home." She walked to where bundles of boughs were piled on the floor.

He followed her. "How can they?"

"You're a good landlord. Their cottages are in repair and the land is well tended." Helen picked up a branch of cedar. "They're eager to see you."

Charles was about deny her assertion when Georgette's voice rang out.

"Look up."

He glanced at the ceiling. They were standing underneath one of the chandeliers. Hanging from it was a Christmas ball of mistletoe.

"You have to kiss."

Chapter 5

Helen's heart skipped a beat.

Charles's lips twisted into a wry grin. "We'd best do as they ask."

For years she had dreamed of kissing Charles, but never with an audience. She took a calming breath. "Georgette can be very determined."

He bent to give her a light peck on her cheek.

Georgette squealed. "Not like that."

"You'll destroy your reputation, Stratton." Rayburn's voice held laughter. "Do it properly."

Stratton sighed and then put his arm around her waist. Her stomach fluttered. He pulled her closer. Helen's breath caught in her throat. All these years of loving from a distance and finally she was in his arms.

His mouth descended and she closed her eyes. His lips brushed across hers. Soft at first and then they settled firm against her mouth. She savored the feel and taste of him. The world spun. Her knees weakened and if he hadn't been holding her, she would have fallen.

Nothing had prepared her for the shock of desire that bolted through her body.

He pulled away and she opened her eyes. She gazed into his dark brown eyes. The world stilled and for a fleeting second she saw the tortured soul within him.

She blinked and the moment was gone.

"Satisfied." Stratton's voice was dry.

Georgette clapped. "It's in the perfect location. We'll catch so many off guard."

"Don't tell me you deliberately set the mistletoe there." Lord Rayburn raised an eyebrow. "How could such an innocent young girl be so devious?"

Georgette giggled. "I may not have been up to London, but village life holds its lessons."

"You shock me." Rayburn clutched at his chest, his voice raised in mock alarm.

Helen stepped back from Stratton. The exchange between Rayburn and Georgette had given her a chance to recover her composure. Her stomach churned and she forced herself to ignore the ache in her chest. A muscle twitched in Stratton's jaw and his eyes narrowed as he watched the wordplay between Georgette and Rayburn.

The kiss had meant everything to her.

Charles looked annoyed.

"What's going on here?" Lady Sybil's shrill voice rang throughout the ballroom.

Helen turned and walked back to the boughs she'd left on one of the side tables. She couldn't face the others right now. Her heart was still beating at a rapid pace and she rested her hands on the table. She took a deep breath and stilled the agony within her chest.

Georgette's giggle brought her back to the present. She forced a smile onto her lips and turned to face the others.

"We're hanging the kissing boughs." Georgette pointed at the mistletoe.

"That is not funny and is in poor taste." Lady Sybil's voice echoed around the ballroom. She turned to Helen. "This is your idea. I should have guessed you would show a lack of taste."

"Miss Bryant had nothing to do with it. I brought the mistletoe." Georgette's voice was indignant. "Everyone hangs them."

"Not in my house. Only a ninny would be caught under one."

"Is that so?" Georgette tilted her head. "I would hardly call..."

Lord Rayburn interrupted before Georgette could finish. "You're being unfair. When I was at the Marquis of Kelvington's London house last Christmas, he had them hanging all over the place."

"He doesn't have a wife to stop him."

"True, but his mother is still alive and she very much approves." Lady Stratton's calm voice came from the doorway. "The villagers love it."

"I knew you would approve." Georgette clapped her hands together. "Last year's mistletoe was stuck in a side corner, but I thought this placement was much better."

Lady Stratton smiled. "You will catch many an unsuspecting couple."

"I find it very strategic." Lord Rayburn grinned. "If anyone wishes to catch me off guard, they're welcome to try."

"You're insufferable." Lady Sybil spat the words at Rayburn.

"Enough Sybil." Stratton's voice was a low growl. "Christmas is meant to be joyous. The villagers and tenants expect to have fun, not a lesson in proper manners."

Helen watched Lady Sybil's eyes narrow and her hands clench into fists. Her face reddened and then she took a deep breath before turning her back on Stratton. She walked toward her.

"You put them up to this." Lady Sybil's voice was a low snarl. "I won't countenance your interference once we're married."

Helen forced her voice to remain calm. "I had nothing to do with the mistletoe placement. If you object that much, I will have Georgette move it to a window embrasure."

"That would be worse." She crossed her arms across her chest. "There would be no controlling the low behavior in a place so private."

"It's done in fun." Helen kept her voice low. "There are no ulterior motives."

"Don't be naïve." Lady Sybil picked up one of the pine boughs that Helen had finished tying into a rope. "This won't last. You don't have enough experience to pull it off."

Helen frowned. "Are you talking about the decorations? We had the gardener cut them this morning. They're fresh."

"Not the boughs. I'm sure they'll do fine." Lady Sybil threw the rope down. "I know you want Stratton, and I won't stand for it."

"You're mistaken. We're friends and nothing more." Helen gripped the bough tighter.

"You don't fool me." Lady Sybil lifted her chin. "My sister found out that you're one of Stratton's tenants. I won't allow you to live there once we're married."

"Lord Stratton was generous to me and my sisters when my brother died." Helen tried to keep the chill out of her voice. "If you have a problem with my living arrangements, then you must discuss it with him."

"I've already told him that things have to change." Her voice quivered with anger. "I won't tolerate his mistress so close to home."

Helen gasped. "How dare you. We're friends, nothing more."

"I'm familiar with Stratton's reputation." Lady Sybil tossed her head. "You're too much of a temptation for him to resist."

"Your words are offensive." Helen picked up the bough and turned to move away. Lady Sybil's hand stopped her. Her fingers tightened on her arm.

"Don't cross me on this." Her voice was a hiss. "I can make life difficult for you. No one will let you into their house when I'm finished. There'll be no chaperoning young ladies, either. Your reputation will be in shatters."

Helen straightened her shoulders. "I'm not without friends. Any scurrilous allegations you throw my way will be seen as lies."

"People will believe me."

"You would accuse your own husband of infidelity?"

Lady Sybil rolled her eyes. "Stratton has no intention of being faithful. He and I both understand the reasons we're marrying."

"Then why concern yourself with me?"

"He can keep his mistresses in London, not here." Lady Sybil threw Helen's arm down. "I've warned you, so have a care. I can ruin you in the blink of an eye."

She spun around and walked over to Lady Stratton. Helen sagged against the table and took a deep breath. She had thought Charles was marrying for love. She pressed a hand against her churning stomach and fought back the nausea. Lady Sybil made it sound as if they were entering into a contract where they would soon go their separate ways.

"Don't let her upset you." Helen jumped at the concerned voice of Lord Rayburn next to her ear.

She forced a smile and turned around. "She thinks I'm a threat to her."

"In her mind, every woman is."

"I've no intention of interfering with her marriage." She picked up the bough and went to one of the oak side panels in the ballroom. There was a hook ready for decorations and she strung one end of the pine to it and then draped it so that it hung down and attached to another hook on the next panel.

Rayburn held the rope while she wrapped it around the last hook. "You're much too beautiful for her peace of mind."

Helen rolled her eyes. "I've been on the shelf for several years. Lady Sybil has no need to concern herself."

"Beauty such as yours does not fade."

She frowned and looked up at Lord Rayburn. "Are you flirting with me?"

He grinned. "I thought you'd never notice."

Helen started back to the table. Rayburn followed her and helped her with the next rope. He was charming and handsome, but her heart didn't beat faster when he was near. There was only one man who could make that happen. And right now he was standing beside his mother glaring at her. She lifted her chin.

"Stratton doesn't like me talking to you." Lord Rayburn leaned close to her. "Why do you think that is?"

She shrugged. "He hasn't spoken to me since my brother's death."

"He warned me away from you."

"I'm capable of handling myself." Helen started toward the next panel. "I've raised my sisters and seen them married. I'm not a young girl in her first season."

"No." Lord Rayburn's voice was low. "You are a woman and that is what makes you irresistible. Why haven't you married?"

Helen stopped at the next hook. "That's none of your business."

"You don't strike me as someone who is looking for a husband." Rayburn cleared his throat. "Perhaps you've loved and lost?"

She looked at Rayburn over her shoulder. "I do not pine for unrequited love. My reasons for not marrying are my own."

"Touché." Rayburn grinned. "You strike me as a person with common sense. Marriage would be the prudent course for a woman."

"You think that because I can see the practicality of it, I would enjoy marriage?" Helen tilted her head. "You're wrong. I decided long ago that I would only marry for love."

"You can't tell me that no man has made your heart flutter?" Lord Rayburn's voice held disbelieve. "All women fancy themselves in love several times before they actually settle on a husband."

"You've forgotten my common sense." She smiled and hung the next bough. "I won't settle for second best."

"You have lost your heart." Rayburn nodded. "A foolish thing to do if your love is not returned."

She frowned. "Why do you think that?"

"You would have married otherwise." Rayburn gave her a twisted smile. "Either he is no longer alive, or he is a fool."

"Neither." Helen walked back to the table.

"Interesting." Rayburn's soft voice sent a shiver up her spine. "You don't mourn and it doesn't sound as if you have regrets or anger. Why?"

"I don't dwell on the past." Her hand paused over the pine bough. "There's too much joy in each day to waste it on regrets. I'm the only person responsible for how I feel, so why would I be angry about loving someone?"

Rayburn tilted his head. "You're serious."

Helen picked up the bough. "I'm not a child who doesn't know their own mind. I'm happy with my life."

"Even without a husband."

She laughed. "Is that so surprising?"

"It's remarkable." Rayburn's voice held admiration. "You're unique."

"You haven't spent enough time talking with women."

Rayburn threw back his head and laughed. "My time with the ladies is not spent in conversation."

"Then perhaps you should try it."

Just then Georgette and Lady Stratton joined them at the table. Georgette held several mistletoe balls in her hands. "Lady Stratton has charged me with finding these a special home. Would you care to help Lord Rayburn?"

Rayburn gave a slight bow. "I'd be delighted."

Helen watched the two of them walk away together. "I hope he doesn't break her heart."

"Rayburn doesn't dangle after young girls." Lady Stratton's voice was soft. "I would suspect you're more his style."

"He's a charming man, but I have no intention of losing my head over him."

Lady Stratton ran a finger over the pine needles that littered the table. "I'm concerned that you might do something foolish because of Charles's engagement."

Helen looked up. Lady Stratton had been a good friend and advisor over the years since her own mother had died. They had never openly discussed Charles in the past, but she was certain that Lady Stratton had guessed long ago how she felt about him.

"I want Lord Stratton to be happy." Helen's voice was low.

"We both do." Lady Stratton's tone was sympathetic. "He is marrying for the sake of the succession, not love."

"That doesn't mean it won't be a successful marriage." Helen cleared her throat. "Many have wed for less."

"True, but Charles needs someone who can help him. The war altered him."

"It changed all of us."

"Some more than others." Lady Stratton picked up one of the boughs and handed it to her. "My son may have healed physically from his battle wounds, but he still carries the mental scars of war."

Helen glanced over at Charles. He was speaking with Lady Sybil and frowning. Her chest tightened. She had hoped his engagement meant that he had put the past behind him. Now she wasn't so certain.

"Once he's a father, he'll have to move forward."

"I pray that you're right."

Lady Stratton walked to one of the wall panels and Helen followed with another decoration. They hung the bough and ribbons in silence. It was usually a joyous occasion when they were decorating the ballroom, only marred by the absence of Charles. Today, he was here, but a gloom hung over the room.

"Lady Sybil won't allow you to stay."

Helen grimaced. "She has already made that clear."

Lady Stratton clasped her hand. "What will you do?"

"Now that my sisters are married, I shall find a cottage near one of them." She kept her voice steady. "Julia has spoken of one in a village near her."

"We shall miss you."

"And I you." Helen smiled. "It was inevitable that I would leave."

"What's this talk of leaving?" Stratton's deep voice sounded behind her.

Both she and Lady Stratton turned. His brow was furrowed. Helen's heart started to beat at a rapid pace. She tightened her hold on the bough to resist the impulse to soothe the frown from his forehead.

"Julia has found a cottage for Helen."

"What's wrong with the one you have?"

"It's perfect." She forced her voice to remain steady. "With my sisters starting families of their own, they want me to live closer."

"Surely you can travel to them?"

Lady Stratton moved away. The last thing she wanted to do was discuss her living situation with Charles. She'd hoped he'd be too busy with the preparations for his marriage to notice her move. He had ignored her existence for the past eleven years, why would this be any different?

"It's best I move."

A muscle in Stratton's jaw clenched. "Lady Sybil has said something to you. I gave the tenancy of that cottage to you for life. My marriage has nothing to do with it."

"It changes everything." Helen didn't hide her exasperation. "Your fiancée is uncomfortable with the arrangement."

"I can deal with her."

"There is no need. I'm leaving."

Chapter 6

Helen took a deep breath of the crisp winter air as she walked down the familiar forest path. The pines were laden with snow and their branches were decorated with icicles. Nature had prepared the landscape for the holidays. Her heart ached as she tried to memorize the beauty of the trees. This would be her last Christmas at Stratton.

She had to see their childhood hideaway one last time.

It was an old game keeper's cabin that Jack and Charles had used as their secret place. She had always tagged along after Jack. They grumbled about her being there, but she'd been allowed to stay. It had become her secret sanctuary too.

Since Jack's death, and Charles's desertion from Stratton, she'd been the only one to visit the old cabin. In their childhood it had been a haven; a place where make believe and fairy tales existed. Now its memories were bittersweet. She pulled her spencer closer to her body as a shiver raced through her. Life hadn't turned out how they'd planned when they were children.

That was a time when anything had been possible. There was no death, no injuries and no heartbreak. The future had held hope. Reality was harder to deal with. She shook off her depressing thoughts. She'd never been one to dwell on the negative. Life was too short for that.

Her feet crunched through the thin layer of snow on the ground as she neared the old cabin. It was stone with a thatched roof. Charles and Jack had claimed it as their own when they were ten. The walls had been falling in on themselves and the roof was non-existent. They'd spent most of that summer repairing the hut with materials that they'd scrounged from the estate. Every year afterwards they'd made improvements until they'd left for Cambridge.

She was within twenty feet of the small cabin when she sniffed the acrid smell of burning wood. A stream of gray smoke swirled above the chimney. Footsteps in the snow coming from the opposite direction, led to the door. Someone was in the building. No one ever visited it except her, so there was only one explanation.

Charles was there.

She hesitated a second. The cabin was on Stratton property, and she doubted he would want someone intruding on his privacy, especially her. She had planned to visit it one last time before leaving, but she could do that tomorrow before the fete. She turned to go home when a horror-filled shout ripped through the air.

It had come from the cabin.

She picked up her skirts and ran to the door. She flung it open and stood in the doorway, squinting, until her eyes adjusted to the dimly lit room. It took a few seconds before she could make out the figure of Charles. He was sitting with his arms on the table and his head resting on them. His shoulders quivered and his head was moving back and forth. He was asleep.

She shut the door behind her and walk over to him. She bit her lower lip as she stretched out a hand to shake him awake. He might not thank her for intruding, but he couldn't continue with the nightmare he was having. Her fingers fluttered against the shoulder of his green riding jacket before she gripped him and shook.

He shrugged and pulled away.

She shook harder. "Wake up."

Stratton lurched back from the table and sat upright. His eyes flitted around the room before they settled on her. "What are you doing here?"

"I heard you yell."

He ran his fingers through his hair. "I must have fallen asleep."

"Do you have nightmares often?" Helen pulled off her gloves. "It sounded as if someone were killing you."

"They were." Charles grunted. "I relive that day constantly. The day Jack died."

A wave of nausea swept through her and she grabbed the back of one of the other chairs at the table. Stratton watched her with a raised eyebrow as she sat. She'd had so many questions about her brother's death, but there had been no one to ask.

"You've never spoke about it." She couldn't hide the tremor in her voice. "Were you with him?"

"I never left his side." Stratton sat back in his chair. "We were retreating when a volley of shots flew over us. I was hit in the leg. When I looked back, Jack was on the ground."

Helen clasped her hand together in her lap. "He'd been hit?"

"There was blood everywhere." Stratton's voice was low. "I grabbed him. We were so close to our lines. All he had to do was come with me."

"How bad was he hurt?"

Helen's stomach clenched into a knot. It had been so many years ago, but she still needed answers. This was the last day her brother had been alive. Any information about his death would be a solace. For both their sakes, she needed to hear about Jack's last minutes of life.

"I couldn't tell where the bullet had gone in." Charles looked up at her, his eyes haunted with memories. "There was no stopping the bleeding. I tried to get him to come with me, but he wouldn't move. He said he was finished."

"It must have been horrible."

He nodded. "He was my best friend. We did everything together, but he laughed. He said this was one time when he'd do it alone."

"He knew he was dying."

"Why didn't he try?" His voice cracked. "I would have helped him."

"You were injured too." Helen reached out and touched his arm. "You had to get yourself to safety."

He pushed away her hand. "I would have traded places with Jack."

"He knew that."

"Did he?" Charles moved back from the table. "Did he also know what his dying would do to his family?"

"We survived." She frowned. "Surely you don't blame yourself?"

"It was my fault." He spat the words at her. "You lost your home and had to raise your sisters. You never had a chance to have a life of your own. It should have been me who died that day. No one cared if I lived."

"I cared."

"You?" Charles's voice was a whisper. "How could you? You have more cause than anyone to blame me for Jack's death. You begged him not to join up with me."

"That doesn't mean I hold you responsible because he died." Her voice was gentle. "How could you ever think that I would have wanted you dead?"

"You must hate me."

"Never."

"I destroyed your life." His voice was hoarse. "I took away any chance you had to be happy."

She smiled. "I'm content."

"No. I saw your face the first time I returned to Stratton after Jack's funeral."

"I was in mourning." Helen kept her voice steady. "I didn't blame you for Jack's death."

"All these years I thought you couldn't bear the sight of me." He slumped his arms onto the table.

"You never stayed long enough to speak to me."

"I couldn't risk your condemnation." Charles clenched his fist. "I was the reason Jack died and you were forced out of your home."

"Jack chose to join up." Helen enunciated each word as she held his gaze. "He wanted to go with you."

"He'd still be alive if I hadn't suggested it."

"You don't know that." She put her hand on his arm. "Jack was restless. He wanted adventure. He was too young to take on the responsibilities of the estate and the family."

"You were forced to instead."

"True, but I never once regretted raising my sisters." Helen frowned. "Did you think my life was ruined because of them?"

"What about Bessington?" Charles raised an eyebrow. "My mother told me you refused his offer. If you hadn't been in shock over Jack's death, you would have accepted him."

"I didn't love him." Her voice softened. "My decision not to marry had nothing to do with Jack's death. How could you possibly think that?"

"I blame myself." A muscle in his jaw tightened. "If I hadn't included Jack in my mad scheme to join the army, he'd still be alive."

"You had no control over what happened." Helen's voice was insistent.

"I pushed Jack to join."

Her eyes widened as she looked at him. For a second her heart seemed to freeze and then began to race. Realization dawned on her. She'd thought he hadn't cared about anything, when the reality was, he cared too much.

"So you've carried this guilt all these years. Is that why you stayed away from Stratton?"

"That and the nightmares. The war left its mark on me." A shudder went through him. "Some days I couldn't bear to face myself."

Helen's heart constricted at how he'd punished himself. He had let his torment build up to such a point that he couldn't even bring himself to come home. Charles's injuries may have healed, but the scars he carried from the war were deep.

She cleared her throat. "Have you talked to anyone about this?"

"Men don't discuss such things." He closed his eyes for a second. "I've learned to live with it."

"By accepting that the nightmares and horror will be with you always?" Helen winced. "That doesn't sound as if you're coping very well."

Charles shrugged. "I control it for the most part. Coming back to Stratton has made everything worse."

"You can't stay away from your estate for the rest of your life. You're getting married. You'll have children and they'll want to be brought up at Stratton, or do you intend to leave them here with your wife?"

He snorted. "You don't know Sybil very well if you think she'd stand for that. She values her position in society too much to bury herself in the country."

"So you both want to live in London." She clenched her hands together on her lap. "It sounds as if you'll be perfect together, but what happens to Stratton?"

"You think we'll be happy?" He gave her a twisted grin. "I'm marrying her because it's past time that I had a wife. I need an heir and my mother has been very patient with me all these years. I can't keep disappointing her."

"There must be something you love about Lady Sybil."

"What does love have to do with marriage?" His voice was filled with loathing. "We both know what we want from this alliance. Once I have an heir, we plan to go our separate ways."

His words pierced her heart. How could he speak so coldly of marriage? She'd accepted that she would never have a husband and family. She didn't dwell on it. There was too much happiness and joy in her life to feel cheated. Her solace was believing that Charles was happy. Now she realized that he had been imprisoned in his own private hell.

"If you had to wed, why didn't you ask me?" Tears pricked her eyes. "At least I love you."

Charles inhaled a sharp breath.

Too late, Helen realized what she'd admitted. The words were out before she had a chance to think. She straightened her shoulders. There was no point in denying how she felt. She had loved him for too long.

"How can you?" His voice was hoarse. "I ruined your life."

Tenderness swelled within Helen. He was still blaming himself for surviving. She must make him understand the depth of her feelings. She might not be a part of his life in the future, but she could free him from the past.

"I've loved you since I was sixteen." She said. "There's nothing you could do that would destroy my love."

"I've made such a mess of everything." Charles groaned. "I've stayed away all these years because I couldn't bear to see hatred in your eyes."

"Now you know the truth." Helen's voice was soft with compassion. "You can let go of your guilt and move forward with your life."

"It's impossible."

"You must." Helen's voice was insistent. "It's the only way for you to be happy."

"You don't understand." Charles held her gaze. "I love you too."

Chapter 7

A wave of dizziness made her grip the table.

She tried to speak, but the words caught in her throat.

"I didn't realize it until I kissed you yesterday." Charles's finger caressed her hand. "I felt as if I'd been kicked in the head and I was awake for the first time in years. Everything was clear. I'd been running away from life and you. I was a fool not to have known sooner."

Tears of joy escaped from Helen's eyes and rolled down her cheeks. She didn't care. She wanted to dance, laugh, and sing all at the same time. Charles loved her. She'd waited a lifetime to hear those sweet words from him. It was pure bliss to let her eyes roam his beloved face.

"I remember the moment I knew that I would love you the rest of my life. You had come to see Jack after you two had been sent down from Cambridge. We were in the stables. I looked around and there you were, arms dangling over the stall wall and a grin from ear to ear."

"All these years and you never said anything?"

"How could I?" Helen turned her hand so that she was holding his fingers. "I was the troublesome younger sister of your best friend. I hoped that one day you would see me as a woman."

"I was blind. I must have loved you my whole life, but I didn't want to admit it."

"The war and losing Jack were too overwhelming for you." Helen now understood his pain. "I wish you had told me sooner how greatly it had affected you."

"What good would that have done?" A muscle tightened in his jaw. "You already had too much to worry about. I couldn't add to your burden."

"I should have pushed you to talk."

Charles gave a short laugh. "When? I was never here. I blamed myself for Jack's death and your straightened circumstances. You were the last person I wanted to see."

She looked down at their clasped hands. "I knew you were avoiding me."

"Why didn't you marry someone else? You could have had children and a good life."

"I know myself too well to settle. It would have been unfair for me and him." She looked up at Charles and smiled. "I enjoy my life. I loved raising the girls and seeing them happy. There's no reason for you to think I've been cheated."

"I failed you." Charles didn't hide his torment. "What am I to do? I can't in good conscious break my engagement. I know I'm a reprobate, but I still have my honor."

"I wouldn't want you to break your word."

"If only I had come home before I'd entered into this travesty of an arrangement with Sybil." He clasped her hand tighter.

"We all come to love in our own time."

"I was slow to understand. You were Jack's sister. I never thought of you as a woman until I held you in my arms yesterday." Charles kissed her fingers. "I've made a mess of my life. Worse, I've made you suffer too."

"What will make me happy is if you make an effort at your marriage. Learn to enjoy Stratton Hall again."

His brown eyes filled with anguish. "Every moment of every day, I'll be thinking of you and what a mess I made of everything. The temptation to reach for you will be too great to resist."

She cleared her throat. "That's why I am leaving."

"No. I couldn't bear it."

"It's the only way you stand a chance of a successful marriage. You want children and I want that for you too."

"How can I consummate my marriage to Sybil?" His voice was filled with loathing. "I feel nothing for her."

"I'm sure it's not the first time you've made love to a woman you didn't care about." Helen's voice was dry.

He grimaced. "You've heard about my life in London."

"It was hard to avoid the gossip."

"So your advice is to ignore how I feel and carry on as before?" Charles pulled his fingers away from her. "I'm doomed to living in this hell."

"You need to talk about your nightmares."

"What's that going to do?"

"You've kept it all inside of you and that hasn't helped. It's made it worse" She hesitated a second before continuing. "Excessive alcohol isn't wise either."

"It helps me forget."

"You have to try something different."

"What's the purpose? I've tied myself to a loveless marriage and lost you forever."

"There are still reasons for you to get better." Helen's voice was insistent. "You'll have children and the estate. They'll both need you."

Charles rubbed the back of his neck with his free hand. For a few seconds she thought he was going to refuse. He was a man of honor and no matter how they felt about each other, he couldn't break his engagement. The only thing she could do was go away and pray that he found a reason to try and get better.

He looked up at her with resignation in his eyes. "What should I do?"

Relief surged through her. "Start focusing on what you can do for the estate. Throw yourself into your work here."

"Sybil won't like it." He gave her a lopsided grin. "She wants to be a big society hostess and that means spending most of her time in London."

She lowered her voice. "I wish I could be near to help you, but that wouldn't be wise."

"At least I know you don't blame me for Jack's death." His voice was hoarse.

"You shouldn't feel guilty because you're alive either." Helen watched a shadow pass over his face. "If you had died, I wouldn't have survived it."

"Even though I deserted you?"

"You were hurt and confused." She stood up from the table and walked to a small window near the door. "Now that you know what the problem is, you can start to get better."

"By talking?" Doubt was evident in his voice. "Who do I speak to?"

"What about your friend Lord Rayburn?"

"He's never been in battle. I doubt he'll understand."

"Then find someone who's been through the war, or speak to Reverend Black. He's a good listener."

"It's been years since I've been inside a church."

"Then it's time to start." Helen went back to the table and picked up her gloves.

"Where will you go?" Stratton stood.

She shrugged. "I've thought about staying with Julia. Her husband has a cottage on his estate that he'd be willing to rent to me."

"Will you be happy there?"

She smiled. "I don't dwell on the past. Julia will soon have children and I can be part of their lives. I'll still be able to travel to my other sisters too."

"It's not the life I envisioned for you." Charles's voice was filled with remorse. "I always thought you'd be married with a family of your own."

Helen swallowed back the lump in her throat. "I refuse to marry just for the sake of it. If we can't be together, then I'll be happy living near Julia."

"I'll be miserable."

"You must try." She walked to him and clasped the lapels of his jacket. "Promise me."

He looked down at her, his brown eyes glittered with desire. "I will, but I need something from you."

"What?" Her voice was a hoarse whisper.

"A kiss."

Her breath caught in her throat and her heart began to race. He pulled her close and her hands flattened against his chest. His face swam in front of her and then he touched her lips.

The world disappeared as her body soared. His mouth fluttered against hers; a soft caress before he deepened the kiss. A jolt of electricity seared through her and she moaned. The next instant, his tongue slipped between her lips and she shuddered with the sensations that burst within her.

He explored the inside of her mouth with a hunger she couldn't resist. She slid her tongue against his, luxuriating in the delicious tendrils of heat that spiraled through her. Never had she felt such a surge of passion and love. It was like coming home after years spent in the desert. She couldn't let him go now.

His hands roamed down her back. She moved against him and rejoiced as she felt his body harden in response. His hands moved up her side and brushed against her breast. Pleasure shot through her and settled in her womb. Her body shivered at the intensity of it.

Charles's lips left her mouth and began to kiss and nibble down her neck. Her spencer blocked him from moving further down. His fingers ripped at the buttons of her coat, pulling it from her body, while his lips continued to roam her face and neck.

Desire burned through her.

He smoothed his hand over her breast and then pushed it out of the bodice of her dress. His tongue licked and tasted every curve before he took the nipple into his mouth and suckled. Ecstasy filled her. She clung to his shoulders to prevent herself from falling.

Her body hummed with need.

She trembled with exquisite joy.

Never in her wildest dreams had she imagined such bliss. His expert lips were sending her into a world of unknown delights. She had loved him for years and never considered the physical act of love. It was devastating. His embrace, the feel of his body, and the smell of him were like a drug. She would crave him for the rest of her life.

The sharp crack of a log dropping in the fireplace broke the spell.

Their lips parted. Helen's heart slowed at the misery she saw in his eyes.

"I was insane to touch you." Charles rested his forehead against hers.

"I never knew such pleasure existed." A tremor went through her.

"It was perfection." His breath was coming in gasps. "It's as if the world was tilted before and now it's right side up."

Helen touched his chin and looked into his eyes. "Thank you. I will always remember this moment."

"How am I going to live without you?" His voice was a hoarse whisper.

She stroked a finger down his cheek. She was shattered. She'd been given the gift of Charles's love only to have it torn from her. There was only one thing left to cling to. Honor.

"We could never be truly happy if you jilted Sybil."

"She doesn't care for me."

She pulled away from him. "She'd be distraught if you walked away from your commitment. You have to remember the estate and your future children."

She started to adjust the bodice of her gown. His eyes never left her. Heat suffused her cheeks and she turned away to finish straightening her gown.

"Don't hide from me." His voice was a husky plea.

"I can't dress when you look at me like that." Helen turned when she was presentable. "You make me long for things I don't understand."

"Passion is like that." Charles's jaw tightened and he took a step back. "My only regret is that I can't teach you more."

"It wouldn't be wise." She swallowed the lump in her throat.

"I could never dishonor you. I love you too much."

The agony in his voice caused her to blink back tears. "I need to get back to the cottage."

"It's almost dinner time."

"Tomorrow is the Christmas celebration." She picked up her spencer from the floor and slipped it on.

"How can I bear seeing you and knowing we can't be together?" His hands clenched into fists at his side.

"That's why I'm leaving right after the fete."

He frowned. "You don't intend to stay for the dinner party?"

Helen lifted her chin. She didn't want to hurt him, but she had to do what was best for both of them. The longer she delayed, the worse it would be.

"I've hired a coach to take me to Julia's for Christmas. After your marriage I will arrange for movers to pack up the cottage and send me my belongings." She forced herself to continue despite the horror she say in his eyes. "Tomorrow will be the last time we'll meet."

Chapter 8

Charles surveyed the crowded ballroom. Every person within ten miles of the estate had come to the party. He stood taller as he saw the genuine joy his tenants showed at having him home. Their acceptance and pleasure reaffirmed his desire to live at Stratton. His eyes scanned the room until they rested upon the one person he wanted to see. She alone was responsible for freeing him from his guilt.

Helen.

She was standing amongst the village children handing out small presents. He remembered from past Christmases that they were usually wooden toys, knitted hats, mittens, or rag dolls. His mother had helped with the making of the gifts in the past. Helen probably helped her now.

What a fool he'd been. He'd wasted years of his life trying to ease the pain he carried from the war. It had taken one afternoon with Helen to make him see his actions had made it worse. If only he'd come home after the war instead of running away.

His guilt had prevented him from speaking to Helen. He'd blamed himself and had assumed she did the same. He wasn't proud of the life he'd lived for the past eleven years. He could and would make changes, though. He was still a man of his word and he would honor his pledge to wed Sybil.

A part of him would die, though.

In a perfect world, he would have realized how much he loved Helen before he'd proposed to Sybil. He would have come to his senses and begged her to forgive him. Instead, he had wallowed in his guilt and refused to come home. So many wasted years. Years in which he could have shared a life with Helen.

"Have you seen Lady Sybil?" His mother's voice brought him back to reality.

He looked down at her. "I thought she was with you."

"She opened the fete with me." Lady Stratton frowned. "She left soon after we greeted the first villagers. I thought she'd gone to be with you."

Charles exhaled. Exasperation at his fiancée's behavior was becoming all too familiar. His eyes scanned the crowd again, but she was nowhere in sight. Sybil wasn't thrilled with meeting his tenants, but that would be one of her duties as his wife. If he was expected to honor his vows, so was she.

"I'll find her."

He skirted the edge of the ballroom, stopping to greet the people who detained him. It took several minutes before he reached the doorway. Beaton, his butler was standing there.

"Have you seen Lady Sybil?"

"I believe her ladyship left with Lord Henry several minutes ago."

He frowned. "Which direction?"

"Toward the library."

He nodded and left the room. Lord Henry and Lady Sybil were friends, but that didn't excuse bad manners. The servants would be gossiping about their disappearance and inappropriate behavior if he didn't make light of the situation. The sooner he found the pair, the less fodder there'd be for gossip.

The library was empty.

He checked the drawing room and the breakfast parlor with the same results.

He glanced out the windows to see if they'd decided to go for a stroll, but there was no one there. A light snow was falling and covering the ground with a fresh blanket of white. No footprints interrupted the pristine landscape. They were in the house, but where?

He came out into the main hall and glanced up the stairs. Sybil might have torn her gown and needed to go to her room to repair it. She wouldn't have done that with Henry, though.

Henry must have wandered back to the ballroom. He hesitated a second, before starting up the stairs. He might not like it, but Sybil was his fiancée, and her place was at his side.

The hallway to the bedchambers was empty.

Charles slowed his pace as he walked toward the room that had been assigned to Lady Sybil. It wouldn't do for one of the servants to see him here, but he had no other recourse. Sending a maid to fetch her would only increase the gossip her disappearance was going to create. He might as well continue and damn the consequences.

When he reached the bedchamber, he raised his hand to knock, but voices from inside stopped him. Sybil must be with her maid. He was about to turn away, when a male laugh halted his retreat. For a couple of seconds the significance didn't register. A chill went through him and settled in the pit of his stomach. His jaw clenched. The muscles in his body tensed as fury clawed at his being.

He opened the door without knocking.

Lady Sybil and Lord Henry were in bed together.

Sybil was naked, and sitting on top of Henry. He wrinkled his nose at the smell of sex that permeated the room. There was no mistaking what he had walked in on. The two were lovers.

His eyes narrowed. Sybil was pulling the sheets over her bare body, but she made no effort to move away from Henry. It was Henry who pushed her off him and then struggled to sit.

"How dare you barge in here?" Sybil's tone was indignant.

"I'd say I had every right." Charles pushed the door closed with a soft click. "There's no point in denying what my eyes can see is true."

Henry reached for his pants on the floor beside the bed. "I wanted to tell you, but Sybil insisted we keep it a secret."

"You didn't think I needed to know?"

"It's not as if you've lived a life of celibacy." Sybil rested against the headboard of the bed with her arms crossed over her chest.

"That's not the point." Stratton walked into the room. "We agreed that we would go our separate ways after the children were born."

Sybil shrugged. "We can still do that."

"Did you think I'd be too drunk to notice you weren't a virgin on our wedding night?"

Sybil rolled her eyes. "What difference does it make? We weren't planning on being faithful to each other."

Lord Henry cleared his throat. "I never intended for this to happen. I fell in love."

"How long has it been going on?" Charles's voice was curt.

Lord Henry's eyes skittered away from him. "Since the summer."

Over six months. Charles clenched his hands into fists and fought the urge to punch Henry. "I thought we were friends."

"We are." Henry's tone was apologetic. "I couldn't help myself. Once you were engaged I didn't know how to break it off with Sybil."

"You could have told me. I would never have proposed if I'd known you loved her."

"I never expected her to accept you." Henry's rubbed a hand over his face. "God, I thought she would marry me."

Charles glanced over at Sybil. She had pulled a robe on and he could see her silhouette clearly in the stream of light filtering through the window. Without her stays, her curves were rounder and fuller than he would have guessed. A fleeting suspicion of the true reason for Lady Sybil accepting his proposal flashed through his mind. Outrageous as it seemed, it looked as if he'd been caught in one of the oldest traps.

"You can't give me what I want Henry." Sybil tightened the tie on her robe. "We've discussed this numerous times."

"Things have changed. That's why I wanted to talk to you this afternoon."

Charles snorted. "You have an interesting means of conversation."

"There's no need to be sarcastic." Sybil went to her vanity and started to pin her hair back into place. "I think it would be best if you left Stratton."

"No." Charles spit the word through clenched teeth. "There is no recovering from this. The engagement is off."

"My father will drag you through the courts if you jilt me." Sybil's voice was menacing. "I'll claim you raped me. Your reputation won't hold against such an accusation."

"I won't back you up." Henry's voice was low. "Stratton has every right to call me out for this."

"It would be pistols at dawn if I gave a damn." Charles couldn't hide his disgust. "Why don't you tell us the truth? You need to marry as soon as possible."

Henry frowned. "What are you saying?"

"Don't tell me you haven't noticed something different about Sybil?" Charles sneered. "Perhaps a bit of weight gain?"

Henry looked over at her. Her reflection in the mirror showed no emotion. "What is he talking about?"

She gave Henry a twisted smile. "You always were a bit slow. Why do you think I took matters into my own hands?"

"She's in a family way." Charles crossed his arms over his chest. "That's why she wanted an immediate marriage. She planned to saddle me with your child."

Sybil put her hairbrush down and turned back to them. "What of it? I needed a husband who could provide me with the lifestyle I wanted. I might love you Henry, but I'm not going to tie myself, or our child, to a life of poverty."

His skin crawled. He didn't know if he was more disgusted at Sybil, or his own stupidity. He'd been too indifferent to notice what she'd been planning. She and Henry had been carrying on this affair for months. The engagement hadn't prevented them from seeing each other. They'd even been sleeping together in his own house. It was suddenly clear. The morning he'd caught Henry in the hall, he'd been leaving Sybil's room.

"When did you plan on telling me about the baby?" Charles's lip curled.

Sybil shrugged. "When I couldn't hide it any longer."

"Did you expect me to just accept it?" Revulsion shuddered through Charles.

Sybil shook out a rose colored ball gown. "What choice would you have had?"

His nostrils flared. He turned to Henry. "What about you? Did you plan this with her?"

Henry's eyes hadn't left Sybil's face. His face paled and his shoulders sagged. He turned towards Charles. "I had no idea about the baby. It changes everything."

"You have no money." Sybil's voice was shrill. "We'd be unhappy together."

"I had a letter from my father" Henry's tone was dull and lifeless. "My brother has had an accident."

"How does that change things?" Sybil rolled her eyes. "Your father hasn't been very generous to you in the past."

"This is different." Henry cleared his throat. "Edward fell and was crushed beneath his horse."

"Is he going to live?"

Henry nodded. "He'll never walk and children are out of the question."

"Is there any chance his wife is with child now?" A note of suppressed excitement filled Sybil's voice.

"They waited a month to be certain before telling me." Henry looked down at his hands. "She is not pregnant."

"So your father wants you to marry." Charles's tone was wry. The Duke of Croxton was more concerned about the succession than his son. Who was he to judge? He'd been guilty of the same thing himself.

"That's why I wanted to speak to Sybil." Henry shrugged. "My father wants me to marry immediately."

"You wanted to propose." Charles looked at Sybil. "You won't have to accuse me of rape. Being a Duchess is much more appealing than a Countess."

Sybil bit her lip and looked at Henry with narrowed eyes. "You're certain your father isn't using this to keep you under his thumb?"

"He only cares about the lineage. If he didn't need me, I'd be poor again."

"So you're going to do your father's bidding?"

"I can't." Henry's voice was firm.

Sybil sank onto the bed opposite Henry. Her shoulders were slumped forward and her lip quivered. "You don't want to marry me now."

Henry reached over and clasped her hand. "I wish you had told me about the baby, but that doesn't change how I feel about you."

"Thank you for being honest." Sybil straightened her shoulders and looked at Charles. "Our engagement still stands."

"No." Henry gripped her by the shoulder. "You're carrying my baby. I don't care who my father has picked out for me to marry, you're the only woman I will wed."

"So the Duke has someone else in mind." Charles snorted. "This is a fine mess."

"That's what I came to tell Sybil."

"And you thought I'd want to hear that?" Her eyes flashed sparks of anger. "You were planning on leaving me."

"You had promised to marry Charles." Henry's voice rose. "I was hoping that my brother's condition would convince you to give me another chance."

Charles glanced at Sybil's mutinous expression and knew Henry would have a hard time persuading her. It wasn't his problem, though. He walked to the door. His hand was on the handle when he hesitated and turned to them.

"Whatever your decision, our engagement is over Lady Sybil. You can tell your father you had a better offer or not. I really don't care."

"I never meant to betray you Stratton." Henry's voice followed him out of the room.

He shut the door on the apology. He no longer cared what happened to them. It was doubtful they'd be happy, but at least Henry's child would have its proper heritage. All he wanted was to put as much distance between them as possible. He'd been blind in his choice of a bride and he wouldn't make that mistake again. The vice grip that had held him prisoner since his engagement, released.

He was free.

This time his heart would be his guide.

He moved through the hall and down the stairs as fast as possible. When he entered the ballroom he stood at the doorway and perused the crowd until he found his heart. He took a deep breath and straightened his shoulders. He was a man with a past, but Helen still loved him. He wouldn't fail her.

His eyes caught her gaze. A tingle of awareness raced down his spine. He would only be complete with Helen by his side. They were connected and he'd been a fool to run away.

He straightened his shoulders and walked toward her.

She gave him a quizzical look. He grinned. He was free at last. His heart soared higher as each step brought him closer to his love. Helen clasped her hands in front of her and waited. He moved faster. She was surrounded by people, but he didn't care. What he had to say couldn't wait.

He stopped in front of her and bowed.

"Miss Bryant, I have an announcement to make that is long overdue."

She tilted her head. "Is there something missing from the party?"

"Everything is perfect." His voice was loud enough that the people standing near could hear. "I love you."

Silence met his declaration.

A blush of red spread over Helen's cheeks. Before she had a chance to reply, he grabbed her hand and led her to the area of the room where the mistletoe hung. It was the same spot where he had first touched her. The place where he had realized that he loved her. He swung her around to face him, gathered her close, and kissed her.

He was home at last.

An ear-shattering cheer went up from the guests. He grinned out at the crowd and raised his hand for quiet, before turning back to Helen.

"I find myself freed from my previous engagement." He gazed into her beautiful blue eyes and relished the surge of joy that filled him. "Helen Bryant, marry me."

Chapter 9

It was Christmas Eve and all the guests had gone to their rooms.

Silence was everywhere.

Helen adjusted the tie on the white silk wrapper that had been a wedding present from Lady Stratton. She blew out the candle on the vanity. She was a married woman now. She turned in her seat and stared at the door that connected her bedchamber with Charles. Soon he would be joining her.

Tonight was their wedding night.

Her body hummed with anticipation.

She and Charles were married and could spend the rest of their lives together. After years of waiting, the speed of their wedding had left her lightheaded. Charles had insisted on a special licence and an immediate ceremony. She sensed that he was afraid something would stop them from being together, and she understood. It all seemed too good to be real.

There was a click and turn of the handle and her heart raced. Her mouth went dry. The door opened on silent hinges and her breath caught in her throat.

Charles stood in the doorway.

His robe hung loose about his waist, leaving the broad expanse of his chest exposed. He cleared his throat before shutting the door behind him. Her stomach fluttered and her heart pounded a loud rhythm. There was an ache in her chest when she saw the uncertainty in his eyes.

Her fear disappeared as she stood and walked to him. She loved him. She'd waited years for this moment. Impatience and desire raced through her. Her need to feel his arms around her was overwhelming in its intensity.

He gathered her within his embrace. "It seems like a dream."

"I'm very real." She lifted her face to him.

He brushed his lips over hers, and then with a groan, he pulled her close. His lips became insistent and demanding. She opened for him, letting her tongue glide over his in a deliciously slow movement. Frissons of pleasure skimmed over her body.

The kiss continued as he bent and lifted her close to his chest. The world spun away until he lowered her onto the bed. He moved to leave her, but she tightened her grip around his shoulders. It had been too long a wait. She needed him now and he didn't disappoint. Charles eased himself down beside her and his fingers loosened the ties of her robe, pulling and twisting it until it was free from her body. He had less patience with her night gown. The tie at her shoulder knotted and when it wouldn't give, he ripped it. The tearing of silk penetrated the fog of desire that had held Helen enthralled.

"Let me." Her voice was breathless.

He gathered the cloth and ripped beyond the tie. The material slid from her shoulders and exposed her breasts. A shiver tickled across her skin as Charles's eyes devoured her. He pulled the rest of the gown from her body, and threw it in a heap on the floor.

She giggled. "What will the servants think?"

Charles nibbled across her bare shoulder. "That I'm an impatient groom."

"I've waited too." She pushed his robe from his shoulders. "Take this off."

"Giving orders already?" He gave her a wide grin. "Why don't we agree to dispense with the clothes before bed in the future?"

"It would save on repairs."

Helen ran a hand over his broad chest. She reached down and slid open the tie. The rest of the material fell away from his body and she inhaled a sharp breath at the beauty beneath. He was all lean muscle, with a taut and rippled stomach. Her fingers roamed over his chest and stomach and then she looked lower. Her eyes widened at the size of his engorged member. She ran her palm down its length. He jerked away for a second and then relaxed. A jolt of excitement settled in her womb. Her fingers stroked and then enclosed him tight. She caressed up and down its span until he groaned and moved her hand away.

Charles pushed her back against the pillows. "I have no wish to end this before we begin."

His lips trailed kisses down her neck and shoulders, while his fingers fluttered against her body. Heat burned through her and settled in her inner core. Its intensity increased as his lips moved lower to her breasts.

His tongue flickered across one of her nipples, sending shards of pleasure throughout her body. She gasped as his lips encircled it and then began to suckle. Hunger pulsed through her, twisting her body with its force. Charles held her in place, his mouth and hands continuing to build the flames of need, until she thought she would scream.

His mouth left her breast and moved to the other one. His fingers moved lower until they feathered against the sensitive skin of her inner thighs. Moist heat flooded her. A finger dipped into her, stroking and rubbing until the tension that had been building, shattered. She exploded with a euphoria that she'd never experienced before. When she had floated back to earth Charles had positioned himself above her.

His hands gripped her hips.

"Ready?"

She nodded. He captured her lips in a searing kiss and then plunged deep within her. There was a moment of discomfort and Charles held himself still until her muscles eased. Then he pulled back and thrust again. This time pleasure spread throughout her.

"Now we are truly one." He thrust again.

She moved to meet him.

She moaned with the bliss that filled her. Nothing in her life had prepared her for the delights of lovemaking. She opened herself to his expertise and luxuriated in the spiral of delicious sensations that he was building within her. They moved together, finding a pace and rhythm that built a tightly coiled passion, until it exploded.

Ecstasy pulsated through her.

He collapsed onto her and she held him close. She couldn't bear for him to leave her. She kissed his shoulder and let her hands roam over his back.

"I'm too heavy." His voice was hoarse. He moved to his side, but kept her with him.

"I never imagined anything so beautiful." Helen's words were an awed whisper.

Charles tilted her chin up. His eyes burned with emotion. "I have been with numerous women, but I have never experienced what just happened."

"We were truly connected."

"I can't be separated from you again." He cleared his throat. "I couldn't bear to go back to the emptiness."

She brushed back the lock of blonde air that had fallen into his eyes. "You'll never have to worry about that. I waited too many years to let you out of my sight."

"How could I have been blind to the truth? I was a fool."

"We can't change the past." Helen's voice was solemn. "We must move forward. From this day on, we share all of our concerns. There are no secrets."

He pulled the bed sheets up around her shoulders. "I promise to try and change."

She propped her head against the pillow. "That's all anyone can do."

He sat and swung his legs over the edge of the bed. He bent and picked up his robe and then stood to put it on.

She frowned. "Where are you going?"

"Back to my chambers." Charles knotted the tie of his robe. "I don't want to disturb your sleep."

"I need you to stay."

"I still have the nightmares. I don't want to frighten you."

She threw back the covers and patted the mattress beside her. "I can handle it."

He hesitated a second and then pulled off the robe. "I've never slept the whole night with someone."

"Neither have I." Helen grinned. "It will be a first for both of us."

"Don't say I didn't warn you."

Charles got into the bed and pulled her close. He cradled her head on his chest, letting his fingers comb through her hair. She inhaled his musky scent and let the steady beat of his heart lull her to sleep.

A loud shout woke her.

Charles was thrashing about under the covers and moaning. Helen leaned over him and shook his shoulder. It took several attempts before he opened his eyes. He stared at her with a blank gaze until he was fully awake. Then he grimaced.

"I disturbed you."

"You were dreaming."

Helen snuggled against her pillows and pulled the blankets close. The fire had burnt down low and there was a chill in the air. Their candles had sputtered out, so the dying embers were the only source of light in the room. Charles's face was in the shadows, but she could hear the agony in his voice.

"It's always the same." He pushed his hair off his face. "It never changes."

"You were on the battlefield." She started the story for him.

"Yes, holding Jack in my arms. He'd been shot."

"You were injured also."

He shrugged. "It wasn't serious."

"You almost lost your leg." Helen tried to keep the pain from her voice. "The letters your mother received from the army surgeon were grim. He thought you would die."

"He worried too much." He crossed his arms.

"You were months recovering and then years before you could walk properly." She reached out and touched his arm. Charles moved as if he were going to pull away, and then stopped. "We were so thankful when you recovered and could be sent home."

"But Jack was dead."

"You couldn't prevent that. It was war." Helen turned his face to her. "You have to stop blaming yourself because you lived. Jack wouldn't have wanted that."

He frowned. "How do I do that?"

"We talk about it."

"And you think that will help?"

"You've refused to discuss it for years and that has only made it worse." Helen's eyes didn't waver from his.

He gazed back at her for several seconds before nodding. He pulled her close and eased her head to his chest. His heart beat steady beneath her ear. She longed to look up at him, but knew that he felt safer talking about the battle if she wasn't watching him. His voice was hesitant at first.

"We had retreated to the coast, but the ships weren't there to transport us. That meant we had to stay in Corunna several days. The French found us the day the fleet arrived."

"So you fought."

Charles nodded. "The cavalry was set up as the second flank. Our orders were to protect the harbor so that the army could board the ships."

"And that's when you and Jack were hit."

Helen fought to keep her voice calm. Hearing how her brother died was torturous, but Charles needed to speak about what had happened. It was the only way for him to get past the guilt and grief he carried.

"We held our ground as long as possible. Chaos was everywhere." His voice wobbled. "My leg was pierced by a bullet and my horse went down. I looked behind just as Jack was shot. He fell to the ground and I crawled over to him. There was blood everywhere."

"It wasn't your fault."

"Then why do I keep reliving it?"

"It was a horrible experience and you've bottled it up inside of you." She smoothed a hand over his chest. "Time is the only thing that can make it better."

Charles inhaled a sharp breath. "It's not that easy."

"It's been tormenting you for eleven years. You won't heal right away, but we have a lifetime together and I'll always be here to listen."

His arms tightened around her. "I love you."

Her finger feathered over his chest. A shudder went through him and a stir of excitement settled in her womb. Her tongue replaced her finger, tasting and laving as she moved lower.

"Careful."

"Don't you like it?" Helen's tone was innocent. "You do realize what day it is?"

"Christmas?" Charles's voice was hoarse.

She let her hand move beneath the covers, stroking and kneading his taut muscles until she reached his hardened manhood. She clasped it, letting her hand move down its long length.

"Our marriage is a precious gift." She tightened her grip around him. "I want to make love again."

"It was your first time and you'll be sore. We should wait."

"I've waited eleven years. I refuse to be patient any longer."

He grinned. "As you wish."

Charles pulled her close and captured her mouth in a kiss that seared her to the tips of her toes. His tongue circled hers, sliding and sucking until she vibrated with desire. Passion burned as all sense of time disappeared. She was held close by the man she had longed and yearned for. He had come home at long last, and with him by her side, everyday would be Christmas.

THE END

Author's Note

The Battle of Corunna was on January 16, 1809. The British army had suffered huge losses to the French during the Peninsular Campaign against Napoleon, and were retreating across the north of Spain to the coast. They began their withdrawal on December 25, 1808 and faced harsh winter conditions which resulted in a loss of discipline and order in their ranks. On January 11, 1809, the British reached Corunna, but their transport ships hadn't arrived yet.

The French troops pursued the British and took control of the high ground surrounding Corunna. The British ships arrived on January 14, 1809 and embarkation was started. The British had no intention of holding the port city so they destroyed most of the military stores that they had, including horses, gunpowder, fortress guns, and mortars.

The French were held back at great loss of life to both sides, but in the end the British retreat was completed on the morning of January 17, 1809. The port was left to the French and the Spanish were forced to surrender. Over 900 British soldiers were killed in the battle, including the British commander, Sir John Moore. By the time the troops reached England at least 6000 men were injured or ill.

In total, over 7000 lives were lost in Britain's first expedition into Portugal to aid the Spanish against Napoleon. The British were able to hold the French back at Corunna, but the retreat was a humiliating defeat and left the French in control of Spain.

About the Author

Cynthia Clement is an award winning author who spent most of her childhood with her nose in a book. She began writing stories in her teens, but it wasn't until her forties that she took her writing seriously.

She enjoys ghost hunting, the paranormal, reading and collecting books, quilting, gardening, and great conversation. She has a BSc in Biology, and a BA in anthropology and recently graduated from nursing.

Cynthia believes in second chances, exploring new ideas, and bringing the impossible to life. Her novels, whether contemporary, historical, or science fiction, all focus on love, honor, and intrigue.

She lives in Northern Ontario with her husband of thirty-two years, her teenage son, and two dachshunds.

Website: www.cynthiaclement.com

Books by Cynthia Clement

Science Fiction

aHunter4Hire Series
aHunter4Rescue
aHunter4Saken
aHunter4Life
aHunter4Ever
aHunter4Trust

Historical

The Seduction of Sarah
The Seduction of Madalyn

Novellas
Pleasuring Emily
Christmas Kisses